OTHER BOOKS FROM KANE/MILLER

One Woolly Wombat

The Magic Bubble Trip

The House From Morning to Night

Wilfrid Gordon McDonald Partridge

Brush

I Want My Potty

Girl From the Snow Country

Cat In Search of a Friend

The Truffle Hunter

The Umbrella Thief

Winnie the Witch

First American Edition 1987 by Kane/Miller Book Publishers
Brooklyn, New York and La Jolla, California

Originally published in Norway in 1986 under the title
Farvel, Rune by Det Norske Samlaget, Oslo, Norway
Copyright © Marit Kaldhol and Wenche Øyen 1986

First published in the U.S. by special arrangement
with Breakwater Books, Ltd., St. John's, Newfoundland

Library of Congress Cataloging-in-Publication Data

Kaldhol, Marit.
  Goodbye Rune.

  Translation of Farvel, Rune.
  Summary: When her best friend accidentally drowns,
a little girl, with the help of her parents, tries to
come to terms with his death and her feelings of loss
and sadness.
  [1. Death—Fiction. 2. Grief—Fiction.
3. Friendship—Fiction] I. Øyen, Wenche,
1946-   , ill. II. Title.
PZ7.K12357Go 1987   [E]   87-3330
ISBN 0-916291-11-1

Printed and bound in Singapore by Tien Wah Press Pte Ltd
      3   4   5   6   7   8   9   10

Goodbye Rune

Marit Kaldhol • Wenche Øyen

Translated by Michael Crosby-Jones
English adaptation by Catherine Maggs

 Kane/Miller Book Publishers

Brooklyn, New York & La Jolla, California

As long as Sara could remember, Rune had been her best friend. He lived in the red house just down from hers, next door to her grandparents.

The year Rune first went to school, when Sara was still too young, she waited for him to come home and would not tell her secrets to anyone else. Now she and Rune walked to school together.

Since today was Saturday, when Rune came over to Sara's house, it was to ask her to play.

"Put on your warm jacket," called Sara's mother. "And be careful not to get wet if you go to the lake. It's too cold to play in wet clothes."

As soon as Sara saw the little wooden boat in Rune's hand, she knew what he was thinking. Last Saturday they had pretended the lake was the ocean, and that Rune was a fisherman. This Saturday they had planned to build a shop where Sara would sell the fish. But first Rune would have to go out in the boat and bring back the catch.

"Let's pretend we're married," said Sara. "We have to hug before you leave. That's what Mom and Dad always do."

"All right," said Rune.

They put their arms around each other, and Rune kissed her on the cheek. Then they looked at each other and laughed.

"While I'm gone you look for sticks to build the shop," said Rune.

"All right. I'll see you later," said Sara. "Goodbye Rune."

As she looked for sticks near the shore, Sara wondered whether she and Rune really would get married when they grew up.

"It would be so nice to eat supper together every night," she thought.

Suddenly she noticed that her sneakers were soaking wet. She had been enjoying her thoughts so much that she hadn't realized the high grass she had come to was partly under water.

Sara remembered her mother's warning. "I'd better go home and get my boots," she decided.

Running along the path, she could feel a little warm spot on her cheek.

"That's where the kiss is," she thought to herself.

As she ran back to the lake, Sara was hoping Rune would be back with the catch so they could start building the shop.

She couldn't see him when she got to the lake, but she could see his boat bobbing cheerily on the water.

"Rune!" she called. "Rune, where are you?"

Then she spotted him in the water. He was over between the big rocks. He looked as though he were swimming with his clothes on.

"Rune!" Sara called, running down to the shore. "Rune, come out of the water!"

But Rune did not answer. He was lying face down in the water. He seemed to be looking for something on the bottom.

"Rune!" Sara called again. But there was no reply from Rune, and the only movement was the bobbing of the toy sailboat.

Suddenly in the silence, Sara became frightened. Realizing something was very wrong, she turned and ran for home as fast as she could.

When she came to her street, she began screaming for her mother.

Sara's grandfather, who was working in his yard, caught Sara in his arms.

"Rune!" she cried. "He's lying in the water! He's lying in the water and he won't answer me!"

Quickly the grandfather handed Sara to her grandmother who came out of the house when she'd heard Sara's cries. Then he ran toward the lake.

Sara's grandmother held her tightly. At first Sara struggled to get free, feeling she must go back to the lake. Then she gave in and began to cry. Sobs came from deep inside her. She cried and cried.

"There, there," said her grandmother. She rocked Sara gently but all the while kept her gaze on the road that led to the lake.

Four days later, Sara, in her best dress, was sitting in the living room with her father. She had had so many questions and had asked them again and again.

Once more her father explained that Rune was dead. Probably he had tried to reach for his boat and fallen into the water and drowned. That meant he wouldn't be able to talk any more, or see, or hear. He wouldn't be able to walk, run or play. He wouldn't smile at Sara or hug her, or kiss her cheek, and she would never see him again.

"I won't see him today at the funeral service?" asked Sara.

"No," answered her father. "Rune's body will be in a box called a coffin."

Sara's mother came in to tell them it was time to go.

"Are you sure Rune is never coming back?" Sara asked on the way to the funeral.

"Yes, quite sure," her mother answered. "But in a way he's not gone. If we think about him, we can almost see him inside us. We can talk to him in our minds."

And this was true. Sara discovered she could see Rune quite well inside her head, especially if she shut her eyes. She could see him smiling, just the way he always had. For a moment Sara felt a little better. But when she remembered that she could not play with Rune anymore, her sadness returned.

Nearly everyone from the village had come to the funeral. People were wearing dark clothes, because this was not a happy day. Sara could see Rune's mother and father and his big sister, Ruth, sitting near the front very close together. Even their backs looked sad.

The fine white coffin was covered with flowers sent by Rune's friends. One bunch was from Sara and her family.

The minister entered slowly. He spoke in a slow, sad voice. When the grown-ups stood, Sara did not. She just sat and listened.

Up above a woman was playing the organ. The music came out in great, sad notes which filled the room and seemed to rest softly against the faces of all the people.

Sara sat quite still with her eyes closed, remembering times with Rune.

After the service, Rune's uncles carried the coffin up the hill to the cemetery. Others followed, walking in a slow dark line after the coffin.

In the middle of the cemetery there was a freshly dug hole. Gently the men lowered Rune's coffin into it. The minister spoke again, and when he had finished, threw a little dirt on the coffin.

Sara thought about Rune lying there not moving, not feeling anything. Suddenly another thought came into her mind.

"What if Rune wakes up and wants to get out? What if he can't get the lid off the coffin?"

"Rune won't wake up," said her father. "He won't wake up again."

Sara looked at Rune's mother and father. She could see that they were crying; crying and holding Ruth. She could see how sad they were.

Sara walked over to Ruth and took her hand. "I wish you weren't so sad," she told her.

Ruth didn't answer, but she held Sara's hand tightly.

"You know," said Sara, "if you close your eyes, you can see Rune inside your head. You can even talk to him in your mind."

Ruth nodded, and Sara hoped she felt a little better.

Sara's mother came to tell her it was time to go home. But Sara wanted to look at the coffin just once more.

"Rune is lying down there," she thought. "He's lying there forever, all by himself."

"Goodbye Rune," she whispered to him.

As she walked home between her parents, Sara felt a little warm spot on her cheek. It was wet. It was a tear.

A few days after the funeral, it began to snow, and Sara knew the long winter had set in. She sat by her window and wondered what the cemetery looked like now.

"It must be white and very still," she thought. "The graves must look as though they are sleeping."

Sara's mother had told her that Rune would not feel cold. But it was hard to think of him lying under the snow when they were in their warm house. They made plans to go and visit the grave when spring came.

The winter had been long. But for days now Sara watched the snow melt and run away in little rivers.

When Sara leaned out her window on Saturday morning, she felt the change. The air was mild and soft against her cheek. It smelled sweet and fresh. She could see her mother wheeling her big bicycle out of the garage.

"Come for a ride," her mother called. "We'll go and visit Rune's grave."

Soon Sara was sitting on the back of her mother's bike, her hair blowing in the warm breeze.

When they reached the cemetery, Sara remembered the dark day she had been here. Today the cemetery looked different. For one thing, Rune's grave had a stone on it. It was cool and smooth and pale grey with Rune's name carved in it and some numbers which told when he was born and when he died. And today the sun was shining brightly, and Sara heard birds singing.

"Is Rune still down there?" Sara asked.

"Yes, in a way," said her mother, "but Rune's body is slowly turning into earth."

"But Mommy, Sara said, her voice trembling, "I wish Rune could come back. I want to play with him."

She began to cry. Her mother knelt down and held her in her arms.

"I want him to come back. I don't want him to become earth. I want him here, with me."

Sara pressed herself against her mother. She felt her mother's hands stroking her hair as she rocked her gently.

"But you know he can't, Sara. Rune can never come back to us."

Sara cried for a long time. Then she and her mother wandered hand-in-hand among the gravestones. Sara began to look at the numbers on them. Most of the people buried there had lived long lives.

Bright spring flowers were growing on most of the graves. But on Rune's where the earth had been dug, there were only a few little white snowdrops poking their heads out. Sara picked a big bunch of flowers and placed them among Rune's grave.

"There!" she said. "That's a little present for Rune from me."

"And it's a wonderful present," replied her mother. "Your flowers will leave their seeds on Rune's grave. Next Spring they'll grow right here."

Sara ran her hand over the cool, smooth stone with Rune's name on it, then patted it before turning away.

Sara climbed onto the back of her mother's bicycle, and they set out for home. On the road the wind brushed against her cheek.

Quietly Sara thought about Rune. She leaned forward a little so she could rest her face against her mother's warm back.